For Finn and George, with love ~ M C B

To my Grandfather Hakon Kristensen ~ T M

International Standard Book Number: 978-1-56148-682-3

Library of Congress Catalog Card Number: 2009028318

Original edition titled *One Special Day* published in English by Little Tiger Press, an imprint of Magi Publications, London, England, 2010
LTP/1800/0077/0310 • Printed in China

Library of Congress Cataloging-in-Publication Data

Butler, M. Christina.

The special blankie / M. Christina Butler ; [illustrations] Tina Macnaughton.

p. cm.

Summary: While Little Hedgehog babysits his cousin, with help from his forest friends, Baby's favorite blanket brings them some misadventures but later saves the day.

ISBN 978-1-56148-682-3 (hardcover : alk. paper) [1. Hedgehogs--Fiction. 2. Blankets--Fiction. 3. Babysitters--Fiction. 4. Forest animals--Fiction.] I. Macnaughton, Tina, ill. II. Title.

PZ7.B97738Spe 2010

[E]--dc22

2009028318

The Special Blankie

M. Christina Butler

Illustrated by Tina Macnaughton

Intercourse, PA 17534
800/762-7171
www.GoodBooks.com

Spring was here at last and Little Hedgehog was very excited.

"The sun is shining, off we go —
To find out where the bluebells grow!"
he sang, merrily packing his lunch.

Just then, he heard a voice calling outside.

It was Ma and Baby Hedgehog.

"Could you look after Baby?" asked Ma anxiously. "I must take care of Mole. He has a dreadful cold."

"Oh my!" replied Little Hedgehog. "Of course I can."

"Thank you," she said, giving Baby a big kiss. And off she went.

"We're hunting for bluebells today, Baby," smiled Little Hedgehog.

"Whee!" squeaked Baby Hedgehog, as they set off together. "Baby's hunting bluebells, and Blankie's coming too!"

Badger, Fox and Mouse soon joined them.

"This is my baby cousin," said Little Hedgehog. "He's coming along to help."

"Very nice," nodded Badger, taking the lead.

"A baby?" frowned Fox. "And what's that *thing* he's holding?"

"It's my blankie!" giggled Baby Hedgehog.

"We'll find the best bluebells in Wild Flower Woods," began Little Hedgehog.

"I see one!" squeaked Baby Hedgehog, running off into a bramble patch.

"Baby! Come back!" cried Little Hedgehog.

"Don't worry. He won't be far away," said Badger, as they all began searching through the brambles.

All at once Baby Hedgehog pattered out, covered in leaves. "For you!" he beamed, holding out a big, blue feather.

"Thank you, that's beautiful, Baby . . . but where's your blankie?" said Little Hedgehog.

"My blankie!" cried Baby Hedgehog in a panic. "I've lost my blankie!"

"Oh no!" groaned Fox.

"It's all right, Baby," said Little Hedgehog gently. "We'll find Blankie."

And they began searching the brambles again.

"I found it!" Mouse called out. But as she tugged at the blanket, suddenly the bramble sprung back . . . PING!

BUMP!

Mouse fell on her bottom, and the blanket went sailing up in the air.

"Blankie, come back!" squeaked Baby Hedgehog.

Just as the blanket floated to the ground, Baby Hedgehog dived onto it, and went bumping and bouncing in a blankety ball down the hillside.

"He'll hurt himself. Stop him!" cried Little Hedgehog, running after Baby.

"Here we go again," puffed Fox, joining in the chase.

The blankety ball rolled to a stop and
Baby tumbled out among the primroses.

"Oh Baby!" gasped Little Hedgehog.
"Thank goodness you're safe!"

"Baby likes hunting bluebells!"
laughed Baby, as they hugged each other.

“Would you believe it?” smiled Little Hedgehog. “We’ve reached Wild Flower Woods.”

“Ready, set, go!” Badger cried, and off they ran to see who would find the bluebells first.

"Over there!" Mouse shouted out.
"I've found them . . .

EEEEEK!"

"What was that?" exclaimed Fox.

"It was Mouse!" cried Little Hedgehog.
"Come on! We must help!"

Mouse had fallen into a deep, dark hole.

"It must be an old rabbit warren," muttered Badger.

"Hold on!" called Little Hedgehog. "We'll soon get you out."

Little Hedgehog, Badger and Fox tried and tried but the hole was just too deep to reach Mouse.

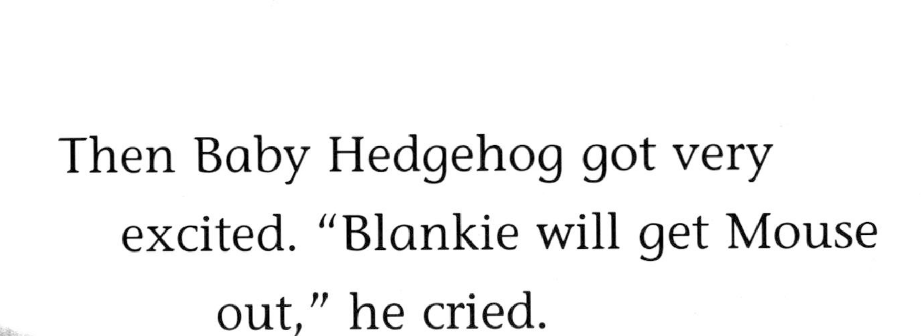

Then Baby Hedgehog got very excited. “Blankie will get Mouse out,” he cried.

“That’s it!” said Badger. “We’ll pull her out with the blanket!”

“Well done, Baby!” said Little Hedgehog proudly.

Little Hedgehog and Baby held on to the blanket tightly and Mouse caught hold of it.

"One! Two! Three! *Pull*!" cried Little Hedgehog. Then everyone tugged, and with one mighty heave . . .

Mouse popped up out of the hole!

"Hurray!" they shouted, giggling and falling back together.

"We found the bluebells," chuckled Badger, "but what a day!"

"And what a hero!" Fox smiled at Baby. "Just like your big cousin, Little Hedgehog."

And chattering and laughing, they all sat down together for a special picnic among the bluebells.